qJP

Ward, Nick, 1962-

Don't worry Grandpa /

AUG 1 1996

8/13/96
6/12/15
(14) no owner

For Audrey

First edition for the United States published 1995 by Barron's Educational Series, Inc.

First published in 1994
© Nick Ward 1994
Nick Ward has asserted his right under
the Copyright, Designs and Patents Act, 1988,
to be identified as the author of this work

First published in the United Kingdom in 1994 by
Hutchinson Children's Books
Random House UK Limited
20 Vauxhall Bridge Road, London SW1V 2SA

Random House Australia (Pty) Limited
20 Alfred Street, Milsons Point, Sydney
New South Wales 2061, Australia

Random House New Zealand Limited
18 Poland Road, Glenfield
Auckland 10, New Zealand

Random House South Africa (Pty) Limited
PO Box 337, Bergvlei, South Africa

Random House UK Limited Reg. No. 954009

All inquiries should be addressed to:
Barron's Educational Series, Inc.
250 Wireless Boulevard
Hauppauge, New York 11788

Library of Congress Catalog Card No. 95-9970

International Standard Book No. 0-8120-9425-5 (hardcover)
International Standard Book No. 0-8120-6533-6 (paperback)

Library of Congress Cataloging-in-Publication Data

Ward, Nick, 1962–
    Don't Worry Grandpa / Nick Ward. — 1st ed.
      p. cm.
    Summary: Grandpa gets nervous when a thunderstorm starts until
    Charlie explains that storms are caused by giants coming out to play.

    ISBN 0-8120-9425-5
    [1. Thunderstorms — Fiction. 2. Fear — Fiction. 3. Grandfathers —
    Fiction. 4. Giants — Fiction.] `I. Title.

PZ7.W21554Do 1995
[E] — dc20
                                              95-9970
                                             CIP
                                             AC

PRINTED IN CHINA
5678   987654321

~Don't Worry, GRANDPA~

Nick Ward

BARRON'S

Grandpa was making tea when a flurry of leaves spiralled past the window. BOOM! the sky rumbled.

"Sounds like a storm brewing," he said to Charlie.

"Never mind, Grandpa," replied the child. "It's time for our story."

Charlie climbed on Grandpa's knee and settled down to listen.

"Once upon a long, long time ago..." began Grandpa. But just then the house shook as the sky gave another, deeper rumble.

"Oh, dear," muttered Grandpa. "I don't like thunderstorms, Charlie. Do you?"

"Don't worry, Grandpa," said Charlie. "It's only the giants coming out to play."

They slam their door and rush outside, leaping and hollering.

"Giants, is it?" laughed Grandpa, patting Charlie's head. "Well, if you see one, you tell him to go home at once."

He put a slice of bread on his toasting fork and held it over the fire.

The sky darkened. CRA-ACK! it thundered.

"Oh dear, it's getting nearer, Charlie," said Grandpa.

"Don't worry, Grandpa," whispered Charlie. "It's only those giants playing marbles."

They send huge boulders rolling and rumbling over the hills, casting their inky shadows as they play.

CRASH! Grandpa jumped as a jagged flame
split the sky.

"My goodness," he wailed. "That was close."

"Don't worry, Grandpa," said Charlie. "It's
only the giants lighting their sparklers."

The sparklers fizz into life. The giants wave them through the air, leaving tails of crackling fire.

WHOOSH! Rain began pouring down and the
wind howled across the countryside.
"Oh dear," Grandpa exclaimed.
"Don't worry, Grandpa," said Charlie. "It's only
the giants playing water chase."

With buckets full to the brim, they romp after each other. Splash! Then they race away, water teeming to the ground below. Trees bend and bow as the giants charge past. The air is filled with the thunder of their footsteps. Their cheers become the wind.

Rain lashed against the window panes and the wind whistled down the chimney. Grandpa sighed deeply. "I have never liked thunderstorms, Charlie," he said.

"Don't worry," smiled Charlie. "Come and have a rest and get warm. I'll read the story, and when I've finished all the giants will be gone."

"Giants, giants? You and your giants," yawned Grandpa as he dropped off to sleep.

Grandpa's bedroom window rattled in the storm. Charlie looked up. "Shhh! Stop your noise," he whispered to the giant. "You'll wake my Grandpa. Go home now."

The giant smiled at Charlie and waved goodbye.

When Grandpa woke up the storm was gone.
The late afternoon sun sparkled on the ground as
Grandpa and Charlie made their way outside
to finish the story.

"Giants indeed," said Grandpa…

"Whatever next!"